Melody and Song

By Tequila Smith

Dedication

To every child whose name carries history, strength, and love —
may you wear it boldly, speak it proudly, and fill it with purpose.

To the families, who pass down stories through names — your
legacy lives on in every syllable.

And to those who dream of making their name known — may you
write it in the stars with the brilliance of your journey.

With pride and purpose,
Tequila Smith

About the Author

Tequila Smith is an experienced educator, author, and advocate for children's limitless potential. With over a decade of teaching experience and two master's degrees in Curriculum & Instruction and Leadership, Tequila is passionate about inspiring young minds to dream big and believe in themselves. As a children's book author, Tequila uses her love of storytelling to craft meaningful tales that resonate with readers of all ages.

Her stories encourage children to embrace their unique strengths, overcome self-doubt, and pursue their dreams with confidence. When she's not teaching or writing, Tequila enjoys spending time with her husband and children, drawing inspiration from their boundless curiosity and resilience. Through her books, she hopes to leave a legacy of empowerment and self-belief for every child who dares to dream.

Other books by Tequila Smith that are already published and ready for the readers to grab:

- Dream Big, Young King
- Wrapped in Gold
- Today, A Princess. Tomorrow, A Role Model
- The Dragon I'm Slaying
- Stand Up Speak Out No Regrets

In a loving family,
where joy ran deep,

Lived twins, a boy and a girl
with names so unique.

Melody & Song, their names
would ignite,

A tribute to the courage of
our ancestor's fight.

Their parents had chosen
those names with care,

To honor a culture rich
and rare.

"Your names have power. They
tell our story, Of resilience, love,
and ancestral glory."

"Melody," said Mama,
"your name means sound,

A rhythm of strength
that's always found.

It's the hum of hope in
fields of gold,

A tune of triumph,
brave and bold."

"And Song," said Daddy,
"your name is strong,

A hymn of freedom,
where we belong.

It's the chants of marches,
the drums of peace,

A legacy sung, a culture
that won't cease."

The twins would listen,
their heads held high,

Their names had roots
that reached the sky.

Each had a meaning,
a purpose, a role,

A spark of our ancestors
stitched in their souls.

At school, some kids would laugh or tease,
"Melody and Song? Such names as these!"

But the twins stood firm,
their voices were proud,

We are not ashamed, so say them allowed!
"Our names are gifts—we wear them with pride,

A story of resilience, a legacy,
far and wide."

"They hold power, as a matter of fact."
"Used to communicate and make an impact."

"Our ancestors used songs to
share and convey,
Messages of hope that still echo today."

PEOPLE GET THEIR LAST NAMES?

A. FROM THEIR FAVORITE COLOR
B. FROM THEIR JOB OR WHERE THEY LIVED
C. FROM THEIR FAVORITE ANIMAL
D. FROM THEIR FAVORITE FOOD
THE HISTORY AND POWER OF NAMES

Later, at school,
their teacher, Miss Lane,

Spoke of heritage and the
power of names.

"Each name holds a story, a
history, a flame,

A truth from our past, from
where we all came."

THE
AN
O

The twins raised their hands,
their voices rang loud,

"We are Melody and Song,
and we are so proud!

Melody brings joy, and Song
brings peace,

Together we honor our
ancestors' feats."

ESSENTIAL QUESTION:
A LONG TIME AGO, HOW DID MANY PEOPLE GET THEIR LAST NAMES?
A. FROM THEIR FAVORITE COLOR
B. FROM THEIR JOB OR WHERE THEY LIVED
C. FROM THEIR FAVORITE ANIMAL
D. FROM THEIR FAVORITE FOOD

Their classmates listened, their
teasing had stopped,

Understanding their pride, their
jaws nearly dropped.

"Melody and Song,
your names are so cool,

A lesson of history;
a gift to our school."

At home, that night,
the twins sat quietly

As Mama and Daddy
shared their story.

"How did you choose these
names for us two?

What made you decide?
Please give us a clue!"

Mama smiled softly,
her voice full of grace,

"Our people have walked
through time and space.

Melody, your name is the
songs they'd sing,

To heal broken hearts &
find hope in spring."

Daddy chimed in, his eyes shining bright,
"Song is the spirit that gives us our fight.

It's the blues, the jazz, the gospel refrain,
Our heritage carried on through joy
and pain."

Our ancestors sang of freedom,
brave and strong,
Hiding messages in each purposeful song.

A whispered tune, a guiding light,
Led them safely through the night.

Their voices rose, both loud and true,
Through work and pain, their spirits flew.

With every note, they stood as one,
Singing of hope until freedom had won.

The twins hugged their parents
with their hearts ignited

I am Melody! I am Song!
Feeling pride in the names they recited

Each letter, each sound,
a gift so divine,

A treasure they'd carry through
space and time.

From that day on, the twins
would proclaim,

"There's power and beauty
within a name!

It shapes who we are,
and who we can be,
A story, a song, a legacy."

Dc
Melody

Melody and Song,
as the years went by,

Found their purpose, as they
reached for the sky.

With their names as their guide,
they'd always know,

The resilience of our people, and
our roots that grow.

So when you hear a name,
remember this,

Each one's a story,
a moment of bliss.

For names hold power,
a culture, a flame,

Shaping the heart and
igniting the name.